For Anna with thanks — and love ~J. H.

To my boys with love ~B. G.

Text copyright © 2002 by Judy Hindley
Illustrations copyright © 2002 by Brita Granström

First U.S. edition 2002

Library of Congress Cataloging-in-Publication Data

Hindley, Judy.
Does a cow say boo? / Judy Hindley ;
illustrated by Brita Granström. — 1st U.S. ed.
p.   cm.
Summary: Children on a farm want to know which creature says "boo," and learn about animal sounds as they search.
ISBN 0-7636-1718-0
[1. Animals sounds—Fiction. 2. Domestic animals—Fiction. 3. Farm life—Fiction.] I. Granström, Brita, ill. II. Title.
PZ7.H5696 Do 2002
[E]—dc21   2001037617

10 9 8 7 6 5 4 3 2 1

Printed in Italy

This book was typeset in Gararond.
The illustrations were done in pencil, watercolor, and crayon.

Candlewick Press
2067 Massachusetts Avenue
Cambridge, Massachusetts 02140

visit us at www.candlewick.com

Does a Cow Say BOO?

Judy Hindley

illustrated by

Brita Granström

CANDLEWICK PRESS
CAMBRIDGE, MASSACHUSETTS

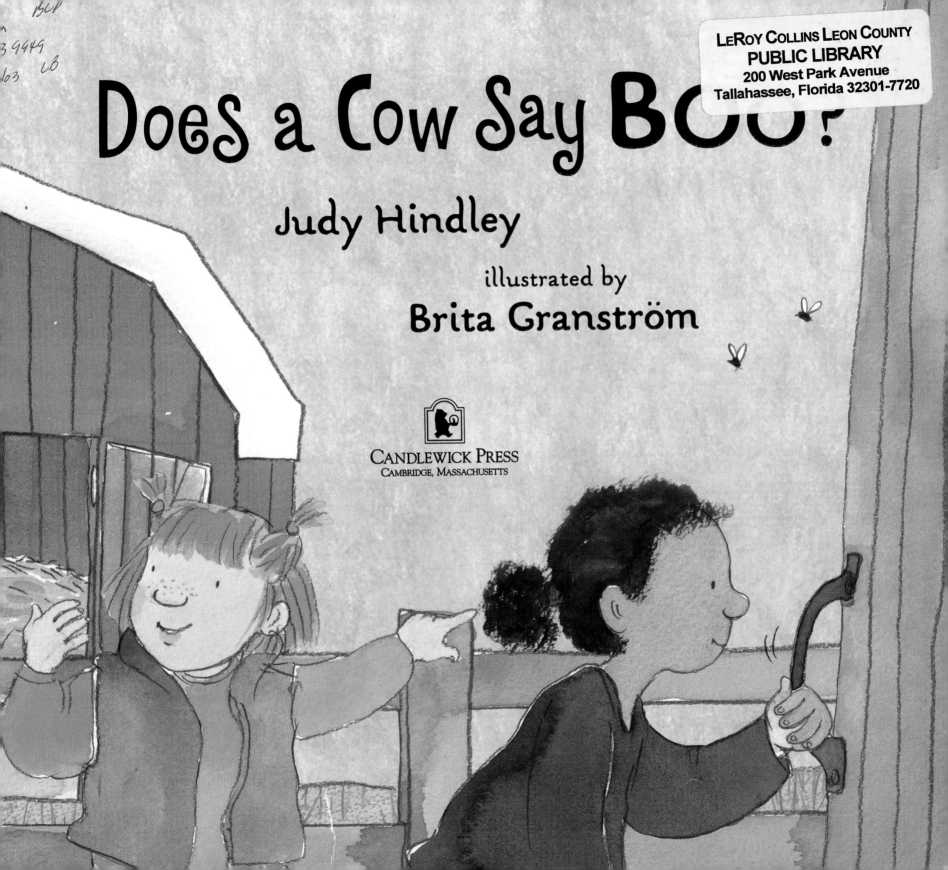

moo!

That's what a cow says—
and you can, too.

So who says BOO?

But who says **BOO**?
Does a dog say **BOO**?

Oh, no!
What does a dog say?

Well then, does a cat say **BOO?**
Don't be silly!
A cat says **mew!**
And a cat says **meow!**

And a cat goes *purrrr* when you stroke her fur.

So who, who,
who says **BOO**?

Does an owl say **BOO**?
No, no, no!
An owl says
whoo—
tu-whit,
tu-whoo!

And down below
a mouse goes
squeak!
A horse says
neigh!

And way up high on the hen house roof
    the rooster throws back his head
        and crows . . .

How does he go?

and her chicks say **cheep,**

a bee goes **buzz,**

a sheep says **baa . . .**

but some little

creatures say nothing at all.

So isn't there anyone who says **BOO**?
Hide your eyes and tell me who.
What do you say now?

You say . . .